For the inspirational, joyful and magical Ellie – thank you!
– T.M.

To Lara and Tamara (of course!), two magical ladies in my life
who have endlessly inspired me.
– E.W.

To those in my life, especially my husband,
who have brought me magic, kindness and joy.
– C.N.D

First American Edition 2021
Kane Miller, A Division of EDC Publishing
Original English language edition first published by Penguin Books Ltd,
20 Vauxhall Bridge Road, London, SW1V 2SA, UK
Copyright © Penguin Books Ltd, 2019

For information contact:
Kane Miller, A Division of EDC Publishing
P.O. Box 470663
Tulsa, OK 74147-0663
www.kanemiller.com
www.usbornebooksandmore.com

Library of Congress Control Number: 2020937022

Printed in China
1 2 3 4 5 6 7 8 9 10

ISBN: 978-1-68464-149-9

Tamara Macfarlane ✦ Ellie Wharton

My SECRET WORLD OF Unicorns

Illustrated by
Ciara Ní Dhuinn

Kane Miller
A DIVISION OF EDC PUBLISHING

The Secret Society
Of Mythical Creatures

Dear Reader,

Hello, I'm Celeste, unicorn seeker and Head of the Secret Society of Mythical Creatures (SSMC). I set up the society when I rescued my first unicorn, Lantern. Unicorns must never be kept as pets, but they do need to be cared for, so I nursed Lantern back to health and returned him to his homeland.

But Lantern is always by my side when I enter the Unicorn World. You can read my story further on in this book.

There are many mythical creatures that need our help – from unicorns and mermaids to fairies and dragons. Caring for them all is far too big a task for me on my own, which is why I need your help. If you're reading this book, you have been chosen to be a unicorn seeker too!

Our role is to find, protect and care for these beautiful creatures. In return, they look after our world. Unicorns are gentle animals that take care of the rivers, forests, meadows and lakes around us. Each unicorn has its own special magical power that it uses to help protect all Earth's creatures.

But there is one very important thing to remember . . . the Unicorn World is a secret. Each magical world is connected to the next by a portal, which is guarded by a gatekeeper. Only children who believe in magic can find these magical portals and meet the wonderful creatures on the other side. If you truly believe, you can learn to be a unicorn seeker just like me. This book will show you how.

Wishing you sparkles of success on your journey,

Celeste

Head Seeker
SSMC

Please follow any safety instructions as shown, and ask a grown-up to help you when you make food for your unicorn.

This is Lantern, my unicorn companion.

He flies all around the world by the light of the moon,
delivering messages to other unicorns and seekers.

Tonight, I have some very important invitations for him
to deliver. It's almost time for our Winter Seeker Party.
Be on the lookout for your seeker party invite.

SEEKING A UNICORN TAKES:

A belief in magic

Patience

Curiosity

Determination

Kindness

Imagination

Oh, and don't forget
some rainbow rounds*
– unicorns can't resist them!

SSH . . . IT'S A SECRET!

Unicorns will only show themselves to a child who is kind,
polite and full of imagination. A seeker must love to sing and
dance and will always be a true friend. Could that be you?

One final thing: unicorns are born in seasons, and all the
unicorns in a season belong to the same family. So, if you are
reading this book in the spring, you may just discover a spring
unicorn in need of your help . . .

* Find out how to make rainbow
  rounds later in this book.

IMAGINE, INVENT, CREATE

MEET YOUR UNICORN

Let's meet your very own unicorn companion. Find your birth month and read the name of your unicorn below!

If you were born in November, your unicorn companion is called Nightfall. If your birthday is in September, your unicorn companion is Coco Caramel.

THE MONTH YOU WERE BORN:

January	Ice Glitter
February	Lightning
March	Blossom
April	Raindrop
May	Mountain Moon
June	Fountain
July	Flame
August	Stargazer
September	Coco Caramel
October	Wild Wind
November	Nightfall
December	Snow Glow

SEEKER SECRETS

Unicorns gather at the end of rainbows; follow a rainbow and you will surely find some.

DRAW YOURSELF MEETING YOUR UNICORN COMPANION

Draw yourself meeting your unicorn for the first time.
You can use these questions to help you create your picture.

Which is your favorite season: winter, spring, autumn or summer?

Which other animals might be around? What do the trees and flowers look like?

Where would you like to meet your unicorn? By a waterfall, in a meadow or by the sea?

What colors do you see in this season?

The Water Unicorn – Keeper of Waterfalls

AQUA

Fact File:

Found in: Waterfalls

Coat color: Aquamarine

Horn, mane and tail color: Silver

Favorite food: Rainbow rounds

Character: Friendly, wise and adventurous

Secret skill: Can speak the languages of all magical creatures

Unique hoofprint: A wave

Mane and tail hairstyle: Waterfall plait

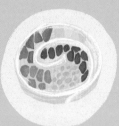

The Rainbow Unicorn – Keeper of Rainbows

PRISM

Fact File:

Found in: Clouds and rainbows

Coat color: White

Horn, mane and tail color: Rainbow

Favorite food: Sherbet shakes

Character: Kind, fair and balanced

Secret skill: Can change the colors of anything that is touched to make the world a brighter place

Unique hoofprint: A rainbow

Mane and tail hairstyle: Dutch plait

COSMOS

Fact File:

Found in: Meadows

Coat color: Hot pink

Horn, mane and tail color: Pale green

Favorite food: Rainbow marble cake

Character: Playful, fun loving and a team player

Secret skill: Can see far across the Unicorn World and into the next

Unique hoofprint: A balloon

Mane and tail hairstyle: Doughnut bun

The Friendship Unicorn –
Keeper of Rivers and Streams

SHANTI

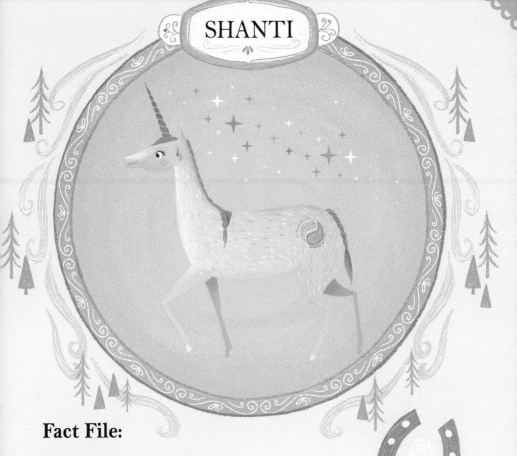

Fact File:

Found in: Rivers and streams

Coat color: Golden yellow

Horn, mane and tail color: Lilac

Favorite food: Cinnamon scones

Character: Gentle, caring and loyal

Secret skill: Can sense danger throughout the Unicorn World and into the next

Unique hoofprint: Clasped hands

Mane and tail hairstyle: Lace plait

BERRY

Fact File:

Found in: Valleys and ravines

Coat color: Raspberry pink

Horn, mane and tail color: Blackberry purple

Favorite food: Fruits-of-the-forest pavlova

Character: Hardworking, patient and organized

Secret skill: Can cry tears that contain the seeds of new trees and plants

Unique hoofprint: A strawberry

Mane and tail hairstyle: Fishtail plait

QUARTZ

Fact File:

Found in: Woodlands and forests

Coat color: Rose pink

Horn, mane and tail color: Lavender violet

Favorite food: Stained glass window cookies

Character: Artistic, creative and expressive

Secret skill: Can sneeze glitter rain that brings happiness to those who see it fall

Unique hoofprint: A diamond

Mane and tail hairstyle: Twist plait

The Sweet Unicorn – Keeper of Crops

SHERBET

Fact File:

Found in: Fields and farms

Coat color: Lemon yellow

Horn, mane and tail color: Gold

Favorite food: Pearl drops

Character: Inventive, generous and quick-witted

Secret skill: Can sniff out food in the most barren of places

Unique hoofprint: A honeycomb

Mane and tail hairstyle: Doughnut side plait

The Festival Unicorn – Keeper of Light
(Gatekeeper of the Unicorn Portal)

LANTERN

Fact File:

Found in: Deserts and savannas

Coat color: Chestnut brown

Horn, mane and tail color: Fire orange

Favorite food: Pumpkin pie

Character: Imaginative, strong and inventive

Secret skill: Can glow in the dark and fly through the night sky

Unique hoofprint: A crescent moon

Mane and tail hairstyle: Loose, flowing waves

The Builder Unicorn – Keeper of Hills and Mountains

BLOSS

Fact File:

Found in: Hills and mountains

Coat color: Forest green

Horn, mane and tail color: Cornflower blue

Favorite food: Moss muffins

Character: Problem solver, strong and confident

Secret skill: A horn that can turn into different building tools

Unique hoofprint: A hammer

Mane and tail hairstyle: Side bun with floral decoration

The Lucky Unicorn – Keeper of Ice and Glaciers

BUBBLES

Fact File:

Found in: Islands and tundra

Coat color: Multicolored spots

Horn, mane and tail color: Arctic blue

Favorite food: Warm sherbet milk

Character: Carefree, daring and a little clumsy

Secret skill: Can blow bubbles through the nose
to protect those nearby from being seen by grown-ups.
The bubbles also make a handy glue!

Unique hoofprint: A bubble

Mane and tail hairstyle: Puffball plaits

ROCKET

Fact File:

Found in: Lakes

Coat color: Jet black with a lightning bolt

Horn, mane and tail color: Silver

Favorite food: Moonmallows

Character: Brave, thoughtful and adventurous

Secret skill: Can collect stardust and use it to guide lost unicorns home

Unique hoofprint: A star

Mane and tail hairstyle: French plait

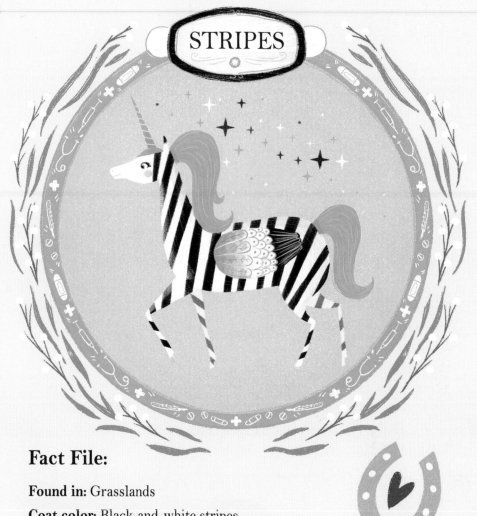

STRIPES

Fact File:

Found in: Grasslands

Coat color: Black-and-white stripes

Horn, mane and tail color: Lime green

Favorite food: Rainbow pizza

Character: Clever, kind and helpful

Secret skill: Can communicate with all animals on Earth

Unique hoofprint: A heart

Mane and tail hairstyle: High ponytail

The Story
of
Celeste

One warm spring afternoon I decided to go and explore the little island where my family had just opened an animal sanctury. I saddled up my rescue pony, Cherry, and headed into the forest. I longed to find a friend and I felt sure that someone was waiting for me there.

I hadn't gone very far when Cherry's ears pricked up. We headed toward a strange noise, following a path through the bracken to a large grassy hill where the sun broke through the trees. A glistening waterfall fell from the high rocky cliffs above. The noise was louder here, and I just knew that it was the whinny of an animal that needed my help. I led Cherry around the edge of the pool of water to take a closer look.

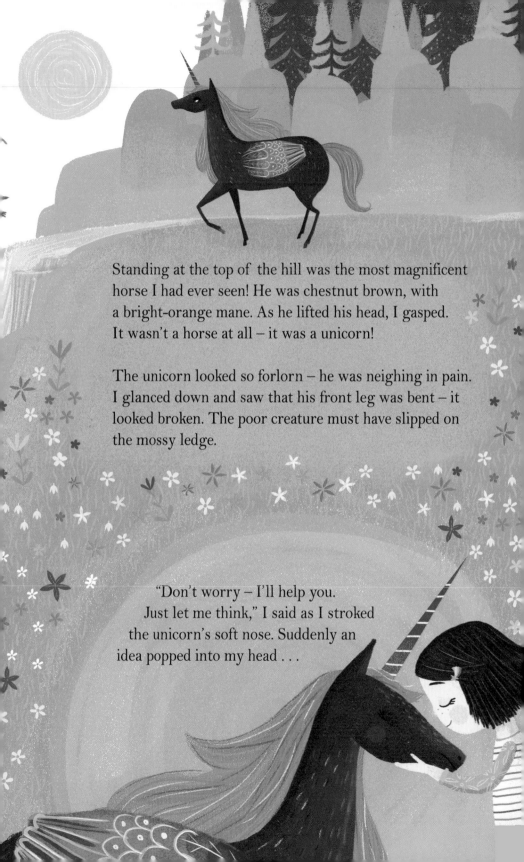

Standing at the top of the hill was the most magnificent
horse I had ever seen! He was chestnut brown, with
a bright-orange mane. As he lifted his head, I gasped.
It wasn't a horse at all – it was a unicorn!

The unicorn looked so forlorn – he was neighing in pain.
I glanced down and saw that his front leg was bent – it
looked broken. The poor creature must have slipped on
the mossy ledge.

"Don't worry – I'll help you.
Just let me think," I said as I stroked
the unicorn's soft nose. Suddenly an
idea popped into my head . . .

On the way to the forest we'd passed a hay cart standing idle in a field. It was just what I needed!

"Wait here and I'll be back before you know it."

I quickly found the empty field and harnessed Cherry to the cart. But making my way back through the forest was much harder now because the afternoon light was fading.

"I'm coming!" I called out, hoping the unicorn could hear. "I just have to be careful in the dark!"

A moment of quiet fell upon the forest, then a soft orange light began to shine, growing brighter and brighter. It revealed a path through the dense trees. I followed it back to the waterfall. The unicorn was still there, but now his orange horn was glowing brightly!

"You clever thing." I smiled. "You guided me back with your magic. I think your name should be Lantern, as that's just what you are."

With Cherry's help, I slowly coaxed Lantern onto the cart with a snack I had brought for myself. They were my favorite – I called them moonmallows – and it seemed that Lantern loved them too!

We hurried home. Once we were safely in Cherry's stable, I wrapped Lantern's leg in a bandage, as I had seen my parents do so many times before.

It was a few months before Lantern could walk properly again. In that time we became the best of friends – we played all day long, and I would groom his mane and tail and sing him to sleep every night.

One day, he was well enough to return home. Lantern had told me that the waterfall was the portal to the Unicorn World, but that I must never reveal its existence. I was sad to see Lantern leave but happy to know that I had made a new friend. I wasn't lonely anymore.

UNICORN SANCTUARY

Back home, Lantern told his friends all about me. The unicorns called me their special seeker as I had sought, found and helped Lantern. It wasn't long before more unicorns turned up at the animal sanctuary seeking my help, and so I became Head Seeker of the Unicorns.

CARING FOR YOUR UNICORN

Keep it **warm**.

While a unicorn is in your care,
it is your job as a seeker to keep it **safe**.

KEEP IT A SECRET!
(It must never
be seen by
a grown-up.)

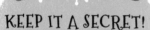

Help it find somewhere
safe to **heal** until it is
ready to return home.

Make sure it has **food**
and **water** every day.

ACTIVITY
Think of other ways
to keep your
unicorn safe.

FEEDING YOUR UNICORN

Unicorns need to eat fruit and vegetables
five times a day, **but** they love sweet
treats best of all . . .

. . . so keep your sweets and cakes hidden
if you don't want them to be nibbled!

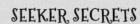

SEEKER SECRETS
Once a unicorn has made you
its friend it will protect you
for the rest of your life.

MAKE, BAKE, DECORATE

RAINBOW ROUNDS

Unicorns can eat all day long. They love anything colorful. Make these rainbow rounds for your unicorn companion.

YOU WILL NEED:

A small container of hummus
1 flatbread or tortilla
2 carrots, finely chopped
1 red pepper, thinly sliced
1 green pepper, thinly sliced
1 yellow pepper, thinly sliced
A cup of grated cheese

Ask a grown-up to help you with chopping.

Yum, yum, yum . . .

INSTRUCTIONS:

1
Spread the hummus on your flatbread.

2
Arrange the vegetables and cheese in strips across the flatbread.

3
Carefully roll up your flatbread.

4
Then cut it into slices.

5
Arrange on a plate and serve to your unicorn.

The Story
of
Josh

Josh loved summer vacation – the sun shone all day long, the trees were covered in leaves, and best of all there was no schoolwork to do! Sitting in the park across from his apartment, Josh noticed something strange on the ground. He brushed the blossoms away to reveal a set of hoofprints. In the middle of each one was a strawberry mark.

That's odd! he thought.

Josh followed the strawberry-stamp hoofprints as they zigzagged over the grass. The prints came to a stop at the leafy curtain of a weeping willow tree.

There, under the umbrella of branches, a beautiful horse lay on a bed of petals. She lifted her head and suddenly Josh saw a horn!

"Are you . . . Are you a unicorn?" he whispered, hardly daring to believe it. He'd always wanted to meet a unicorn!

The unicorn flicked her blackberry-colored mane and tail across her raspberry-pink coat. She looked deep into Josh's eyes and nodded slowly.

"Do you live here in the park?" Josh asked.

The unicorn nodded again. "I'm Berry, and this – " she gestured around with her head – "is my home."

"Why are you so sad, Berry?" Josh asked.

Then he remembered. The park was being turned into a shopping center! The bulldozers had already started to arrive, apple trees were being cut down, and last week the pond had been concreted over to make way for a parking lot. It wouldn't be long before this willow tree disappeared too. Looking into the unicorn's large eyes, Josh knew that there was only one thing to do – he had to save the park!

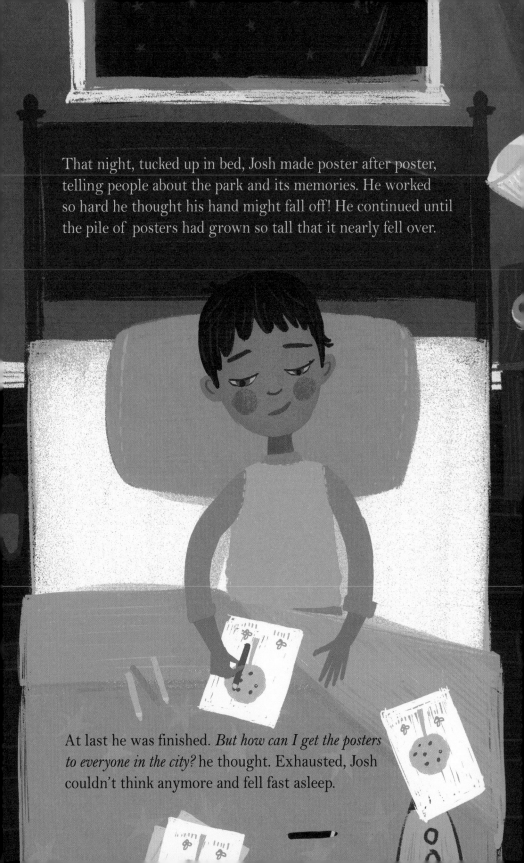

That night, tucked up in bed, Josh made poster after poster, telling people about the park and its memories. He worked so hard he thought his hand might fall off! He continued until the pile of posters had grown so tall that it nearly fell over.

At last he was finished. *But how can I get the posters to everyone in the city?* he thought. Exhausted, Josh couldn't think anymore and fell fast asleep.

He woke a few hours later to a tapping on his window. The unicorn was there, her beautiful raspberry coat twinkling in the moonlight.

"I can help you," she whinnied to him. "Climb on!"

Berry soared above the city with Josh clinging on tightly. When Josh thought they couldn't possibly fly any higher, Berry stopped in midair. With a wave of his arms, Josh flung the posters into the night sky, and watched them drift down toward the houses below, and in through windows and mailboxes.

The next morning Josh and Berry watched as people found his posters and headed toward the park. A large crowd had soon gathered for an enormous picnic. The bulldozers couldn't move at all! The puzzled drivers backed their vehicles out of the park to loud cheers and whoops.

"We did it! The park is safe." Josh smiled.

Berry nuzzled Josh's cheek and he felt her tears on his face. He wiped them away with his hand, and in his palm he saw seven apple seeds.

"Take these seeds," Berry whispered, "and plant them around the park."

Josh found the perfect spot to plant the seeds. Within minutes, little shoots had sprung up everywhere. The plants quickly grew into tall apple trees, laden with fruit.

The crowds gasped in wonder as their park burst into color once again. Josh looked back toward the willow tree. He was almost certain he could make out Berry winking at him before disappearing behind its curtain of leaves.

PLAYING WITH YOUR UNICORN

Unicorns like to play. Here are some
of their favorite activities.

Hoop the loop

Upside-down unicorn rides

Helping other unicorns and animals in need

ACTIVITY
Which other games
will you play with
your unicorn?

HIDE-AND-SEEK
(hiding from grown-ups)

HOOP THE LOOP
(throwing hoops over your unicorn's horn)

FIND AND FORAGE
(helping it forage for berries and apples
– try following a shower of stars)

UPSIDE-DOWN UNICORN RIDES
(handstands)

SPLISH SPLASH!
(splashing in freshwater lakes)

RAINBOW CHASE
(chasing rainbows)

TALKING ABOUT IMPORTANT THINGS
(how to be kind and caring)

HELPING OTHER UNICORNS
AND ANIMALS IN NEED

SEEKER SECRETS
Every year there is a unicorn ball
and the best-dressed unicorn wins
the Unicorn Cup.

GROOMING YOUR UNICORN

You can spend many happy hours with
your unicorn, keeping it looking beautiful.

YOUR GROOMING CHECKLIST:

A unicorn's mane and tail must be washed and brushed every day.

Carefully wash with elderflower soap.

Then brush your unicorn's coat, mane and tail, and pat dry with a silk sponge or owl feathers.

Smooth on glowberry polish.

Once a month, at the full moon, bathe your unicorn in glitter water and rub it down with sugar water.

ACTIVITY
Which hairstyle would you choose?

SEEKER SECRETS
When you brush a unicorn's coat, it glows.

SHERBET SHAKES

Sherbet shakes are a favorite with unicorns. They make them giggle with happiness! Can you make one for your new friend?

Ask a grown-up to help you with the chopping.

YOU WILL NEED:

8 strawberries
2 bananas
1 container of Greek yogurt
A teaspoon of edible glitter
Rainbow sprinkles

INSTRUCTIONS:

Yum, yum, yum. . .

1

Chop up the strawberries and bananas.

2

Whisk them together with your yogurt and edible glitter.

3

Pour the mixture into ice-cube trays and place in the freezer for 2 hours.

4

Once the mixture is frozen, put the ice cubes in a blender to make an icy shake.

Never use a handheld blender and always ask a grown-up for help.

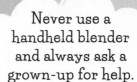

5

Pour your shake into a glass.

6

Spoon some rainbow sprinkles on top and enjoy with your unicorn.

The Story of Jojo

A brisk autumn wind had blown in from the sea while Jojo was out riding her pony toward the cliff tops. She pulled her sweater up to her chin and urged Coco higher and higher with her heels.

As Jojo breathed in the sea air she thought she heard an unusual noise. A sort of whistle. She continued along the coast path, and saw out to sea, on a rocky island, a small horselike creature with a large horn on its head. *Is that really a unicorn?* thought Jojo.

The unicorn looked very frightened, all alone on the island. Jojo needed to rescue it quickly. She cantered down to the beach and began to ready her boat. She picked up the oars and climbed in.

The boat rocked to and fro on the waves. It was hard work
and the wind wanted to pull it in a different direction,
but slowly Jojo drew closer to the little island.

At last the boat landed on the rocky shore with a bump.

Jojo felt the boat scrape against the rocks, but she didn't have time to worry about that. Instead, she ran over to the unicorn and stroked his back soothingly. His multicolored coat felt as soft as petals and his beautiful ice-blue mane and shiny wings glistened in the sunlight.

Back on the boat, Jojo and the unicorn set off for the mainland, but they were soon in trouble. Water was forming a puddle in the bottom of the boat.

"I must have scraped it on the rocks!" Jojo cried. "We're sinking! What shall we do?"

The unicorn whinnied gently and lowered his head toward the hull of the boat. Suddenly there was a rumbling sound and the boat juddered underneath Jojo's soggy feet. She watched in amazement as the unicorn blew bubbles that sealed the hole in the hull.

"Wow!" she breathed.

Quickly, Jojo picked up her oars and rowed for shore. At last they drew near to the beach and she knew that they were safe. She'd rescued the unicorn, but he in turn had rescued her.

Jojo took the unicorn back to her seaside cottage, and as night fell they sat wrapped up in a cozy blanket next to the fire. Jojo sang a lullaby and her new friend drifted off to sleep. As he snored, a huge purple bubble came out of his nose, followed by a red one, then a yellow one, and finally an orange one!

"Your name should be Bubbles!" Jojo laughed. "I'll look after you, and when you're ready you can fly home."

The next morning Bubbles was strong enough to return to the Unicorn World. And Jojo's island adventure meant that she had become the newest seeker of unicorns.

COLOR ME

IMAGINE, INVENT, CREATE

RIDING YOUR UNICORN

When you have gained your unicorn's trust, there is nothing better than going for a ride together.

Two clicks with your tongue and your unicorn will turn left. One click and it will go to the right.

Hold on to your unicorn's mane gently – never pull it.

CLICK
CLICK

SEEKER SECRETS
Unicorns send secret messages to each other by tapping their hooves on the ground.

MAKE, BAKE, DECORATE

MOONMALLOWS

YOU WILL NEED:

A cup of blueberries
A dusting of powdered sugar
A bar of white chocolate,
broken into pieces
10 marshmallows
10 bamboo skewers

INSTRUCTIONS:

1 Wash and pat dry the blueberries.

2 Dust them with powdered sugar.

3 Place them in the freezer overnight.

4 **You must ask a grown-up to help with this step:**
Melt the white chocolate using a bowl of very
hot water with another bowl on top containing
the chocolate.

5 Thread one marshmallow onto each bamboo skewer.

6 Dip the marshmallows into the melted chocolate.

7 Place them on a plate in the fridge to set.

8 Thread your frozen blueberries onto
the marshmallow bamboo skewers.

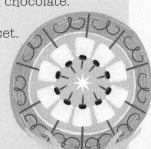

IMAGINE, INVENT, CREATE

A UNICORN LULLABY

Why not write your own secret unicorn lullaby?
Which words make you think of nighttime
and sleeping? Write them down on a piece of paper.
Here are some of mine:

Calm   Stars   Moon   Shhh   Quiet   Rocking

Stories   Softness

Cuddles   Pillows

Cuddly friends   Blankets

Which words make you think of unicorns?
Write them down too. I like these ones:

Glitter   Stardust   Magic   Hooves   Horns

Rainbows   Hay   Peace

Color

Kindness

Happiness

Now - think of your favorite nursery rhyme, for example:

Twinkle, twinkle, little star,
How I wonder what you are!
Up above the world so high
Like a diamond in the sky . . .

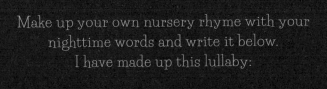

Make up your own nursery rhyme with your
nighttime words and write it below.
I have made up this lullaby:

Softly, softly, here you come,
My magic horse, where are you from?
You're from the clouds and stars and sky,
For you I've made this lullaby!

MY SECRET LULLABY

_____

_____

_____

_____

_____

A UNICORN'S BEDTIME

Unicorns go to sleep when it gets dark and rise with the sun.
They sleep more during the winter months when nights
are longer and days are cooler.

SEEKER SECRETS
Unicorns like to rest their head
on a pillow of clouds. Unicorn
dreams float up into the night
sky and become stars.

They like a bucketful
of glowberry juice to
help them drift off to sleep.

The Story
of
the Seeker Party

Thick snow was falling heavily, blanketing the ground, but inside, beside a cozy fire, Celeste was writing out her invitations for the Winter Seeker Party. When she had finished she gave the envelopes to Lantern, who had instructions to deliver them all that night.

Five nights later it was the eve of the seeker party, and Jojo and Bubbles were flying toward the Unicorn World. Stars filled the night sky, and even more lights twinkled through the distant unicorn portal.

Bubbles flew on and on . . . Soon the smell of cinnamon fruit punch, moonmallows and toasted toffee apples was wafting through the night air!

And what a winter feast it was! The firelight burned brightly as
Celeste, dressed in a beautiful white coat that seemed to be made
of icicles, welcomed her guests.

"Hello, everyone, and welcome to this year's Winter Seeker
Party!" she said. "Our party is in your honor. Let's introduce
ourselves and our unicorn friends first, and then you can relax,
eat and enjoy yourselves!"

There was a small black-haired boy called Jeremiah with his
unicorn, Aqua, who could speak to all magical creatures.
She'd once had afternoon tea with a dragon!

Stripes was a black-and-white unicorn sitting next to a tan boy with long hair called Nico. Stripes could speak to all Earth animals, from monkeys and birds to frogs and wildcats! Jojo watched as Stripes got up and went to greet a pack of wolves that stood watching the party from the edge of the woods.

Sophia was next. When she spoke, her friendly unicorn sent out a shower of sherbet glitter over everyone!

"This is Sherbet!" Sophia laughed.

The last seeker to speak was a little girl with a freckly nose and white hair in a side ponytail. Ella's unicorn was a striking black, with a lightning flash on his flank. "This – " she paused for effect – "is Rocket. He's a winter unicorn who is fond of moonmallows. He is brave and adventurous, but best of all he can guide lost unicorns home using the stars!" Rocket neighed importantly.

It was time for everyone to celebrate and eat. Jojo had never seen so much food! There were rainbow pizzas, sherbet shakes and rainbow rounds galore. Every time a plate looked empty, it was magically refilled! Everything was delicious!

Before bed, Celeste toasted some moonmallows in the dying embers of the fire. Slowly, the seekers and unicorns began to drift off to their tents around the campfire, full of food and very happy. It was a night they would never forget! Being a unicorn seeker was a magical gift indeed.

PARTY INVITATIONS

Why not have your own unicorn seeker party?
Design your invitations and send them
to all your friends!

YOU WILL NEED:

Some sheets of
paper
Colored felt-tip pens
Glitter glue

INSTRUCTIONS:

1 Fold a piece of paper in half.
2 Write the place, date and time of your party on the front
of your invitation.
3 Decorate it with colored pens and glitter-glue patterns.
4 Make enough party invites to send to all your seeker friends.

MY HOUSE
3 p.m. on Friday

SEEKER SECRETS
Unicorns love to dance
and do acrobatics
when no one
is looking.

RAINBOW PIZZAS

Get ready for your party with these delicious pizzas.
**You must ask a grown-up to help with preparing
the vegetables and using the oven.**

YOU WILL NEED:

1/2 cup self-rising flour
1/2 cup Greek yogurt
1 teaspoon olive oil
Some grated cheese
2 tomatoes, sliced
2 peppers, chopped
1 can of corn, drained

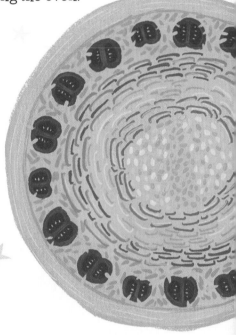

INSTRUCTIONS:

Preheat your oven to 425 degrees.

1 In a bowl, mix together the flour and yogurt to form a dough.

2 Shape the dough into a ball and place it on a floured surface.

3 Knead the dough for 4 minutes.

4 Grease a baking sheet with the olive oil and flatten the dough.

5 Add your favorite toppings - cheese, tomatoes, peppers
and corn are favorites with all unicorns.

6 Ask a grown-up to help you put the pizza in the oven and
cook it for 15 minutes. The grown-up should then take it
out from the oven carefully with oven mitts.

RELEASING YOUR UNICORN

When your unicorn is ready to return to the Unicorn World,
you can help it get home safely.

Pack some of its favorite
food for the journey.

Give your unicorn a keepsake so it
will always remember you.

Make sure the unicorn's hooves are clean
and ready for the walk ahead.

Show your unicorn the way to the waterfall portal.
Don't forget to pack a compass.

WRITE A SECRET LETTER TO GIVE TO YOUR UNICORN

Send a wish to the stars as your unicorn sets off for home.

_____

_____

_____

_____

_____

_____

_____

SEEKER SECRETS
A set of unicorn hoofprints creates a path of daisies as it gallops through a meadow.

WRITE YOUR OWN UNICORN SEEKER STORY

Now that you've learned all about the secret world of unicorns, why not write your own story? How did you become a seeker?

IMAGINE THAT YOU HAVE FOUND A **UNICORN HOOFPRINT**.

A **UNICORN** NEEDS YOUR HELP . . .

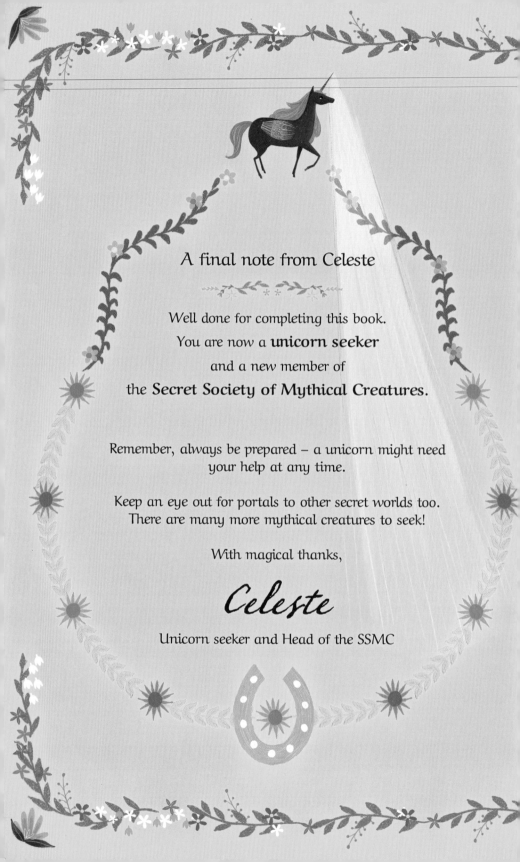

A final note from Celeste

Well done for completing this book.
You are now a **unicorn seeker**
and a new member of
the Secret Society of Mythical Creatures.

Remember, always be prepared – a unicorn might need
your help at any time.

Keep an eye out for portals to other secret worlds too.
There are many more mythical creatures to seek!

With magical thanks,

Celeste

Unicorn seeker and Head of the SSMC

CONGRATULATIONS!

....is a unicorn seeker.

Date I became a unicorn seeker
and a new member of the SSMC ....

My unicorn companion is ....

I pledge to be kind,
be bold, be brave,
and always believe in magic.